An Illustrated History of Japan

text and illustrations by Shigeo Nishimura

TUTTLE PUBLISHING
Boston • Rutland, Vermont • Tokyo

Major Periods in Japanese History

PERIODS	APPROXIMATE DATES	SIGNIFICANT FACTS
Ice Ages	More than 10,000 years ago	Japan is still part of the Asian mainland; people live in caves and hunt animals.
Jomon	13,000 to 300 B.C.	Japan is a series of islands and people begin to live in villages; the world's first pottery is produced here.
Yayoi	300 B.C. to A.D. 300	The last 300 years of the Jomon era co-existed with the beginning of the Yayoi era. Settlers bring rice growing and metal working skills.
Kofun	A.D. 300 to about A.D. 700	Small states develop; ruling classes are buried in enormous mound tombs, called *kofun*—often larger in total mass than the pyramids of Egypt.
Nara	A.D. 710 to 794	A new capital is established. The Buddhist religion increases in popularity during this time and many temples and shrines are built.
Heian	794–1192	Capital moves to Heian-kyo (present-day Kyoto); power of the aristocracy and samurai warriors grows.
Kamakura	1192–1333	The founding of the Kamakura shogunate, with its capital at Kamakura. Emperors reign but shoguns (warlords) rule.
Muromachi	1338–1573	The third shogun moves the capital to Muromachi, Kyoto. Frequent fighting and disorder inspire the construction of huge castles.
Azuchi-Momoyama	1573–1603	The earliest European influences and introduction of guns, which changes traditional warfare methods.
Edo	1603–1867	The capital moves to Edo (present-day Tokyo); commerce and industry develop. Edo became the world's largest city.
Meiji	1868–1912	Japan's rapid modernization following the restoration of the Meiji emperor. The samurais are deprived of their privileges.
Taisho	1912–1926	Advent of radio broadcasting, streetcars, and buses. The Great Kanto Earthquake of 1923 destroys much of Tokyo.
Showa	1926–1989	A military government seizes power and Japan conquers much of Asia; following its defeat the economy rebuilds.
Heisei	1989–	Japan is now the world's second biggest economy after the United States and Japan continues to be a source of new products and ideas.

Long ago, the earth was much colder than it is today. At that time, Japan was still part of the Asian mainland. People lived in caves and survived by hunting animals like elephants and giant deer. These people were the first to live in what is now Japan, more than 100,000 years ago.

The Jomon era following the Ice Ages is when the islands that are now Japan emerged from the sea as world temperatures increased, the ice caps melted and sea levels rose. But Japan was still not a country. Illustrated here is a scene approximately 5,000 years ago. People began to live in

villages. Food was abundant—people hunted wild animals, fished, and gathered nuts and wild plants. They made tools from bones, horns, wood, soil, and stones. Jomon takes its name from the era's pottery—some of the earliest pottery made anywhere in the world.

The prehistoric Jomon era lasted for about 10,000 years. Villages flourished in both coastal and mountainous areas. But there were periods when food was very scarce. People performed ceremonies and prayed to gods for better times. The last part of the Jomon era overlaps with the next

era when overseas settlers and invaders came to Japan. The new emerging social order became known as the Yayoi era and dates from about 2,400 years ago. The Yayoi era lasted for approximately 600 years. Again, this era is named after its pottery.

Approximately 2,000 years ago the Jomon and the Yayoi peoples co-existed and traded with each other. During the subsequent Yayoi era (300 B.C. to A.D. 300) more and more people from the Asian continent reached Japan by boat and these settlers brought new skills—the growing of

rice, the working of bronze and iron, and new religious practices. The new immigrants settled all over Japan, reclaiming swamps, and growing rice. Japanese culture gradually changed and Japan now became an agricultural society.

About 1,900 years ago, the development of canal irrigation meant that rice growing was no longer limited to lowland swamp areas. With bigger rice crops, village populations grew. Villagers cooperated with each other during storms to protect the rice crops and they prayed together for

good harvests. The men in charge of ceremonies and festivals that celebrated good harvests took senior positions in the village, and the village head served as both war chief and shaman. Rice is still very important to the Japanese today as their staple food.

Toward the end of the Yayoi era, around A.D. 200, social classes developed, and parts of the country began to unite under the sway of powerful landowners. Warfare, wealth, and differences in the size and strength of villages were seen. Villages fought one another over water and land.

The victorious villages governed the defeated ones. This is how small nations which ruled one plain or one river basin were born. As a result of many recurring battles, some villages secured control over large areas of the country.

During the Kofun era from A.D. 300 to 700, large mound tombs were used to bury emperors and high ranking aristocrats or nobility. *Kofun* means "old tomb" in Japanese, and native Japanese laborers worked to build these gigantic tombs supervised by Chinese and Korean architects.

From the 6th century onward, the elaborate use of large tombs began to fall out of use by the ruling elite as the result of new Buddhist religious beliefs which did not approve of burial. However in some areas mound tombs were still constructed until the early 7th century.

The Nara era began in A.D. 710 when the Japanese emperor founded a large capital city at Nara. During this period foreign culture, art, and architecture arrived via the Silk Route, the commercial trade route which linked Japan to Europe and China in ancient times. The Buddhist

religion became popular in Nara and splendid temples were built by craftsmen and workers from the provincial areas. But the luxurious life of the emperor and the aristocrats came at a price—heavy taxes in rice and labor needed to be paid by farmers.

In A.D. 794, the capital moved from Nara to Kyoto. The reasons for this are not totally clear. The most likely reason was to reduce the influence of the Buddhist religion that had developed in Nara. This period is known as the Heian era, because at that time Kyoto was called Heian-kyo,

the "City of Peace and Tranquility." The power of the aristocratic families continued to grow, and life in the areas where they lived centered around their huge residences, lavish social gatherings and colorful ceremonies.

During the Heian era, all kinds of people lived in the capital of Heian-kyo—merchants, craftsmen, robbers, and beggars. The city streets were crowded and festive parades often took place along the major thoroughfares. The capital prospered but life was uncertain for most people and

was often short due to disasters and epidemics. A uniquely Japanese cultural identity now emerged with the development of a written Japanese language and a new painting form—the picture scroll, where the picture and story unfolded as the viewer unrolled the scroll.

The importance and influence of the samurai warrior class grew during the Heian period. *Samurai* is the Japanese word for warrior and also means "one who serves." The samurais were paid by powerful aristocrats to protect the land. Gradually they developed into private armies

attached to local warlord aristocrats. They formed into units of samurais and developed a master-and-servant relationship with stronger samurais. They trained extensively and were equipped with arms, armor and horses. At this time, the bow was the preferred battlefield weapon.

Toward the end of the Heian period, two military clans—the Minamoto (or Genji) and the Taira (or Heike)—had grown so powerful that they seized control over the country and fought wars against one another for supremacy. Illustrated here is a bitter battle between the two clans.

The Minamoto defeated the Taira, and in 1192, Minamoto Yoritomo became shogun, the highest military officer and ruler of Japan. He set up a military government at Kamakura independent of the emperor and he was the first shogun to rule Japan under military law.

The Kamakura era from 1192 to 1333 was an age of shoguns (warlords) and rule by the militaristic samurai class. Japan was controlled by a series of military governments or shogunates for about 700 years after this. A prosperous merchant class also emerged at this time and with

increasing trade, more towns developed around seaports, important shrines, and temples. Illustrated here is a typical scene from this era—bustling trade and the development of a riverside commercial town.

The Muromachi era began in 1338, so named because the third shogun, Ashikaga Yoshimitsu, established his residence in the Muromachi area of Kyoto. At that time village life centered around farming and the cultivation of rice. Villagers cooperated with each other in the planting and

harvesting of rice. They held meetings in the village shrine and decided amongst themselves what the local rules would be—how to share things like water, and when and how to celebrate festivals.

The Muromachi era, also known as the Ashikaga Shogunate, lasted from approximately 1336 to 1573. This period saw frequent rioting and a series of civil wars with people fighting for control of the land. When farmers were pressed to repay loans or to pay heavy taxes, riots and

looting would erupt. Toward the end of the Muromachi era riots seemed to break out nearly every year and had an impact on the power of the shogunate. As the Ashikaga Shogunate declined in power, Japan entered an era of civil wars.

During the last years of the Muromachi era from 1467 to 1573, the daimyos (regional lords) were free to do as they pleased, without having to worry about a central government. They were the independent rulers of areas they controlled and many battles were fought over land. Frequent

fighting inspired the construction of large castles. Earlier castles were just places to retreat to during conflicts but now they had living quarters. Farmers were ordered to build the castles. Castle towns developed with the castle at its core and merchants and craftsmen living just outside.

The Azuchi-Momoyama period from 1573–1603 marks the dominance of two shoguns, Oda Nobunaga and Toyotomi Hideyoshi, who built large castles at Azuchi and Momoyama. The first Europeans (Portuguese and Spaniards) arrived in Japan by sea in the 16th century, bringing

Christian missionaries and gun traders with them. The advent of guns meant traditional warfare methods changed. Nobunaga encouraged trade with the foreigners but his successor, Hideyoshi, feared the impact of Christianity.

Under the rule of the Tokugawa family from 1603 to 1867, the capital was moved to Edo (present-day Tokyo) while the emperor remained in Kyoto. Edo became the world's largest city. The Tokugawa family continued to hold power for nearly 250 years. Daimyos (warlords) in the

provinces had to regularly travel to and stay in Edo to demonstrate their loyalty to the shogun. Trade with all countries was cut off except with China and Holland, who were only allowed to trade at the port of Nagasaki. The shogun wanted Japan to remain free from outside influences.

During the Edo period new farming techniques and new kinds of fertilizer increased the quantities of rice harvested, and other crops—such as cotton and rapeseed—were also introduced. There were now more regional differences as to what was grown—cotton being mainly grown

around the city of Osaka. In some areas an additional crop like rapeseed could be grown and harvested before the land was needed for rice. Illustrated here is rice being cultivated and harvested. Buckwheat was also grown and eaten in the form of noodles.

During the 19th century, other industries also developed, such as mining, forestry, and fishing. The Japanese have a long history of whaling, and from the 17th century the technique of net whaling developed; boats formed a semi-circle around the targeted whale and drove it toward shore

where it became entangled in a large net. Using this method, about 150 whales were caught every year but by the end of the 19th century, with the introduction of modern harpoon cannons, the catch increased tremendously. The Japanese use all parts of the whale.

During the Edo era the regional lords or daimyos had to travel to Edo regularly so the road system improved and many inn towns developed, providing shelter for travelers. The roads were also used by merchants to transport commercial goods. The main road from Edo to Kyoto was

the most important and busiest road during this time. Rice, paid as a tax, and other regional products were loaded onto river boats that sailed to the port at the mouth of the river; there they would be reloaded onto bigger boats and taken to Edo or Osaka.

Edo (present-day Tokyo) was the world's largest city from the late 17th to the early 19th century with a population of over 1,000,000 people. Edo flourished as the political center of the Tokugawa Shogunate. Half of its population were samurai, who were virtual bureaucrats, and half

were engaged in commerce and industry. Osaka was Japan's most prosperous commercial city. In both cities, many shops lined the main streets and cheaper apartment houses lined the narrow sidestreets behind the main streets—where servants, craftsmen, and poor peddlers lived.

Wealthy merchants in 19th-century Edo and Osaka loaned money to the daimyos, and when the shogunate and the daimyos fell deeply in debt, more taxes were imposed on the farmers. This sparked revolts and even some samurais attacked the shogunate. But the revolts were violently

quelled and rebellious farmers were severely punished. Japan was still a medieval, totalitarian military society but it was becoming increasingly difficult to maintain the closed-nation policy. Europeans were on Japan's doorsteps with strongholds in China and throughout Asia.

The closed-door policy had to be abandoned in 1853 when Commodore Matthew Perry arrived from America at the port of Shimoda, at the southern end of Edo Bay, and demanded the opening of Japan to foreign commerce. The shogun had no choice but to give foreigners access to

the ports. Many historians consider Perry's arrival as a trigger that caused the downfall of the Edo Shogunate. Eventually, after a period of civil war, the shogun stepped down, and in 1868 the emperor announced the official return of imperial power. This is known as the Meiji Restoration.

During the Meiji period from 1868 to 1912, Emperor Meiji became the head of state and the modernizing impact of Western influences and technology became very clear. Under the instruction of foreign experts, railways and modern communication systems such as the telegraph were

built. The Tokaido Railway was completed in 1889 which ran almost parallel to the route of the Tokaido Road. Western-style buildings and traditional Japanese thatched wooden houses were built in the same areas. Even dress was affected and Western clothing became popular.

The Meiji emperor moved his residence from Kyoto to Edo, now renamed Tokyo, meaning "Eastern Capital." By 1871 the daimyo domains had been surrendered and transformed into prefectures. Rapid modernization took place, including the development of a navy and army, railroads,

factory and steel production, and a parliament. The government wanted a strong military force and conscription was introduced. After winning short wars against China (1894–1895) and Russia (1904–1905), Japan emerged as an international military power.

Emperor Taisho took the throne when the Meiji emperor died in 1911. Japan entered World War I (1914–1918) by declaring war on Germany. This era was a period of tremendous economic development with the advent of radio broadcasting and the rapid increase in the numbers of

buses and streetcars on Japanese city streets. But the Great Kanto Earthquake of 1923 destroyed much of Tokyo and most of old Edo (Tokyo) is now gone forever. The Taisho emperor died in 1925.

In 1936, military leaders gained control of the government and Japan signed a pact with Germany. Japan invaded China and, in December of 1941, Japan bombed Pearl Harbor and the United States entered World War II. Japan then went on to invade the South Pacific Islands and

56

Southeast Asia. With America's entry into the war it was only a matter of time before Japan was defeated and forced to withdraw from the lands it had conquered. Toward the end of the war, Japanese cities were firebombed and Tokyo was again destroyed.

The United States dropped two atomic bombs on Hiroshima and on Nagasaki in August, 1945, and the Japanese quickly surrendered, thus ending World War II. This was the first time that atomic bombs had been used in warfare. Soon after Japan surrendered, it was occupied by